For Iz & Jo!

ISBN 978-1-338-31441-0

12 11 10 9 8 7 6 5 4 3 2 1   18 19 20 21 22 23

Printed in the U.S.A.   40

First Scholastic printing, September 2018

Designed by Maria Elias
This book is set in Trade Gothic LT Pro/Monotype.
The illustrations were created with a #2 pencil and painted in Photoshop.

FALL IS FOR SCHOOL

ROBERT NEUBECKER

SCHOLASTIC INC.

Fall is time for school!

That really is uncool.

Fall is here! It's time for school!
The summer's in the past.

I'm staying here. I will not go.
Vacation went too fast.

Fall is time for turning leaves;
the weather's growing cool.

**Fall is here! Come on with me!
It's time to go to school!**

School is really not my thing.
You go on alone.
I'll be fine all by myself,
sitting here at home.

Let's go and meet your teacher;
you're going to look so nice.
Tuck in your shirt and tie your shoes!

You must take my advice!

Teacher! Teacher? Sister, no!
I do not think that I can go!

In school we'll learn of Romans,
who really were no dummies,
and the pyramids in Egypt,
all filled up with mummies!

Dinosaurs and carnivores,
mighty tyrannosaurus,
giant tigers, woolly mammoths

really were enormous!

I am going to play all day!
It doesn't matter what you say!

Recess is for playing games:
We'll run and jump and climb!
Let's go right now and join the fun.
You really must not whine!

Whine.

Do your numbers! 1, 2, 3!
Add, subtract, and multiply.
**A million, trillion—my, oh my!
Count the stars up in the sky!**

I do not like arithmetic!
It hurts my eyes!
It makes me sick!
I will not go, I do not care.
I have heard enough.
To tell the truth,
I'm not like you.
School is just too tough.

Rocket ships that fly to Mars,
music, sports, and art.
These are all the things you love. . . .
I think you're very smart!

We will learn to read and write;
the stories we will tell!
And if you want to do it right,
you have to learn to spell!

Fall is time for parties,
for spooky Halloween.
We'll dress up just like zombies
and paint our faces green.

In science we will never stop
until we ace the pumpkin drop!

Pumpkin drop?

Pumpkin drop!

We pad them up and drop them.
It's really engineering.
If your pumpkin doesn't smash,
the teacher will be cheering!

Is that something I can do?
And everyone is going?
Staying home day after day
was getting kind of boring.

Fall is time for school!

We'll learn, and we'll be clever.
A great big world will open up
and change our lives forever.

Maybe school will be all right.
I might just reconsider.
Maybe you are not so dumb, for my baby sister.
Fall is time for school!

School is full of awesome!
The world is mighty cool.
It's an amazing universe!
Fall is time for school!